WARNING

This book contains sexually explicit scenes and adult language. It may be considered offensive to some readers. This book is for sale to adults ONLY.

* * * * * * * * * * * * * * * * * * *

Please store your files wisely where they cannot be accessed by underage readers.

DISCLAIMER

ISBN-13: 978-1987863536
ISBN-10: 1987863534

Other Books by Darla Dunbar:

<u>The Romeo Alpha BBW Paranormal Shifter Romance Series</u>

Amanda Walker thinks that she has a normal and boring life. That is until after her 24th birthday. Everything changes when she meets the man who says he was supposed to be her husband. Denying everything the man says, she fights him every step of the way. But after he kidnaps her, Amanda discovers that there are some things about her family that her parents kept a secret all these years. Among the history of the family she learns secrets she thought only happened in story books. Can Amanda tell the difference between truth and lies or is she this mysterious woman that holds the key to a legacy?

<u>Romeo Alpha Blood Lines Romance Series</u>

Twenty-four years have passed in relative peace for Amanda and Romeo. They've raised five children into adulthood and are thoroughly enjoying their lives as the Alpha King and Queen of the werewolves. At twenty-four, Sarina is just stepping into her powers and will be ripe for mating when her birthday comes in two weeks. What no one knows is the danger that lurks just outside their tight knit community. Romeo has made peace with the other clans and has enjoyed that peace, but it will all come crashing down around him when his oldest daughter comes of age to take a mate.

The Alpha Feud BBW Paranormal Shifter Romance Series

Eliza's life consisted of reporting on boring, crowd-pleasing events, like their country livestock fair. With the arrival of two handsome brothers, the lives of Eliza and her best friend, Melissa, are shaken to the core. For Eliza, the arrival of this new man becomes a test of her relationship with her current boyfriend, who she's been happily living with for over six years. Does Hayden, a complete stranger, really wield the power to make Eliza reconsider her relationship with Andrew?

The Alpha Packed BBW Paranormal Shifter Romance Series

Darlene has led a quiet life since suffering through a terrible break-up. She wants nothing more than to spend her time in front of the TV, away from any sort of trouble. But all that goes down the drain when handsome, rugged and rough Idris comes into her life. He is a werewolf on the lookout for his missing pack leader. Darlene quickly finds herself pulled towards this mysterious man and at the same time finds herself falling deeper and deeper into the world of the supernatural.

The Mind Talker Paranormal Romance Series

Ananda finds herself on the run and she's not alone. With help from Jared, a stranger that she just met, the two evade capture by an organization that is intent on hunting her kind. Ananda and Jared are able to read minds. When an unfortunate incident happened involving a disturbed individual that resulted in the death of his schoolmates, the secret organization decided to take action.

<u>The Leather Satchel Paranormal Romance Series</u>

Valtina is stuck in Middle World, unable to pass on to The Afterlife. In order to redeem herself from past deeds done, she must help bring romance back into the world and stop The Dark Side from destroying love in its entirety. Following orders issued by Ladaya and armed with a leather satchel filled with the appropriate tools and weapons, Valtina embraces each mission with enthusiasm.

Get the latest update on new releases from the author at:

https://darladunbar.com/newsletter/

This book is Part One of "<u>The Daemon Paranormal Romance Chronicles</u>"

Book 1 - The Awakening

Phoebe grew up not knowing her mother. The stranger, Apollo Mikos, claimed to know her mother. After that day, Phoebe's life would change forever.

Book 2 - The Shifter

Phoebe is surprised when her dog, Ace, shows up from nowhere. She is on a mission with Apollo to kill the Qilin. That is the only way that the true leader of daemons will emerge.

Book 3 - Forgotten

Juno has been stirring up trouble that has prolonged the infighting among the daemons. In order to get her to stop, Phoebe agrees to give up a year of her memories. But making deals with a siren is never a good thing. Without her memories, Phoebe's romantic relationship with Supay no longer exists. Instead, she leaves Supay for Apollo.

Book 4 - The Siren's Trap

The unsuspecting couple, Phoebe and Supay, made a deal with Juno to stop the infighting among the daemons. But at what price? An entire year was wiped clean from Phoebe's mind. Now Phoebe was with Apollo. Desperate to get her back, Supay considers Juno's new deal. Is it worth the price to pay for the dubious result? To win back Phoebe's love, Supay will need to be unfaithful to her.

Book 5 - Exposed

Hiding away in Peru, Supay and Phoebe start their own family, away from the chaos and the daemon infighting. Meanwhile, Apollo, heart-broken and lost, is lured into another one of Juno's schemes. Making deals with a siren never turns out right. If Apollo accepts the deal, the love of his life may resent him for the rest of his natural life. If he doesn't take the deal, she is lost to him forever.

Book 6 - The Beginning

As preparations for the war between daemons are underway, everyone must begin to choose. Siding temporarily with Apollo, Juno has a moment to look back on her life and figure out how she arrived at this moment. As she sifts through memories of the past, a specific dark stranger stands out. How far will young Juno go with her new love? More importantly, will her mother, Circe, discover the secret tryst?

Book 7 - The Treachery

Having broken the cardinal rule of the sirens, Juno must take action to save her own life and the life of her unborn child. In order to keep her secret safe from the sisterhood, she must kill her lover and conceal her shame. Will Juno betray the sisterhood and save her lover or will she remain loyal by slaying him instead?

Book 8 - Duplicity

Juno's mother, Circe, discovers her lies and gives her an ultimatum to fix everything. As Juno races against the clock to protect her loved ones from Circe, she makes a final choice that could leave her perpetually unhappy. Left to wander the world alone, Juno realizes that freedom means nothing if there is no one to share it with. The nature of Juno's vendetta—and the means she achieves it with—are finally revealed.

Book 9 - Reconnaissance

As Juno's hunt for the daemon's fortress unfolds, Apollo is left alone wondering if she will truly return to him. Will Juno be able to resist her base instincts? More importantly, will she be able to get to the fortress and return without being spotted? Discover how Juno's stealth mission works out.

Book 10 - The Interrogation

Juno tries to hide her rising fear in the presence of her captors. As her fear mounts, she holds on to the hope that Phoebe or Supay will take pity on her. Before that can happen, she has to come clean to Supay about her past. Could he possibly forgive her for what she has done? Will Juno remain faithful to Apollo or will her siren urges take over? Discover how the confrontation with Supay unfolds.

The Daemon Paranormal Romance Chronicles

The Awakening

Book One

By Darla Dunbar

Copyright Revelry Publishing 2015

Table of Contents

Chapter One

THE LAST customer of the day was slowly leaving. Phoebe reached down to pet her dog, Ace, and moved to close up shop. Since graduating high school, she had worked in fairs across the country as a fortune teller, saving money. She did not know why, but when she touched somebody's hand, she could read their thoughts. Although she could not divine their future, she could make educated guesses that were enough to bring customers back. After saving enough money, she had finally opened up her own shop.

Removing the scarf from around her hair, Phoebe let her red curls cascade along her shoulders. Ace sniffed at some of his dog food while she reached over to grab her purse. Before she could close up, a knock at the door surprised her. In front of the door, she saw one of the most gorgeous men she had ever laid eyes on. Curious, she opened the door and let him in.

"Hello! How can I help you, Mr...?" She paused and waited for him to respond.

"My name is Apollo Mikos. Pleasure to meet you, Phoebe Williams." The blonde-haired man reached for her hand and shook it. Instantly, a vision arose before her eyes of Apollo and her rolling around in bed sheets. Waves crashed outside the window—a storm was brewing. As the vision of Apollo entered her body forcefully, Phoebe pulled her hand back. The vision went away, but it left a slight blush on Phoebe's cheeks. Reading the minds of other people was occasionally embarrassing and often felt like a major invasion of privacy. Still, she found herself wishing that she could have held his hand a little longer to see where these thoughts took her.

Motioning toward the table and chairs reserved for clients, she asked if he wanted to sit down. Apollo just shook his head.

"I need your help with something, but not like that." He shrugged his shoulders. Tall and well-built, Apollo had blue eyes and chiseled features. He wore a dark black suit that made all of his muscles ripple beneath the fabric.

Confused, Phoebe looked over at him. "What do you mean?"

Sighing, Apollo looked into her eyes. "You will probably want to sit down for this." Still uncertain, Phoebe sat down and waited for him to speak again.

Gazing out the window, Apollo framed his thoughts. "I know your mother, Rhea. I also know what you really are and I need your help."

Phoebe was aghast. "What do you mean? I don't have a mother. I grew up in foster care after my mother left me there when I was two."

Apollo shook his head. "Before you were born, your mother was raped. They never found who did it and Rhea lived in constant fear. Soon, she discovered that she was pregnant with twin girls. She planned on naming one Cassandra and the other Phoebe. Due to stress, genetics, or just bad luck, Cassandra was stillborn. For a long time, your mother managed to hold it together and take care of you. From what I've heard, the trauma of the rape and having to see a reminder of it every day was too much. She gave you up. The added stress of losing a daughter caused her mental state to break, and she checked into a mental institution."

Leaning back in the chair, Phoebe tried to take it all in. This stranger was telling her things about her life that she didn't even know.

"How do you know all this? And if it's true, where is my birth mother?"

"I know you must have a lot of questions, but for the moment, I need your help." From the back of the room, Ace growled slightly. Phoebe didn't notice the growling, but Apollo shot a wary eye at Ace.

"What could I possibly do? How do I know that you are telling the truth?"

Apollo shrugged. "I could take you to your mother and she could tell you. Then, we can move on to the step where you help me."

The desire to meet this mystery woman who had given birth to her so long ago was too much. Phoebe nodded her assent and grabbed her jacket. Leaving Ace at the fortune teller's hut, she got into the car with Apollo. As he opened her door, her hand brushed against his arm. Reading his mind again, she saw an image of herself thrown back onto the table and Apollo drawing a knife down her body. It didn't look threatening in the vision. Instead, it looked like some type of foreplay.

Sighing, Phoebe pulled back her hand and got into the car. She occasionally saw sexual fantasies about her in thoughts of other men, but Apollo certainly had the most focus. As the car started, she turned to Apollo. "So, what is the rest of the story that you needed to tell me?"

Looking over at her as he drove, Apollo bit his lip. "I honestly don't know whether it's better for your mother to tell you. What do you want?"

Phoebe motioned toward him. "I'd rather find out now if that's possible." Nodding, Apollo began his tale and cautioned her not to interrupt until the end.

When the world was new, there was a wide variety of species created, and humans came in many forms. During this time, a specific kind of human known as a daemon came into being. These daemons each possessed a god-like trait. These abilities included shape shifting, contacting the spirit world, or moving things using only their minds. From these daemons, legends about gods were created. To the average people, daemons were superhuman.

Bickering and constant conflicts broke out among the daemons. To settle the dispute, they made a deal that each family of daemons would rule their own territories of the world. Since each family tended to have certain kinds of abilities, this was reflected in the mythology of the region. For people like Apollo and Phoebe, mind reading, mind control, and prophecy were just a regular part of life. Their family of daemons had moved over from Greece one hundred years ago.

In keeping with the tradition of their people, each baby was named after a figure in Greek mythology. Phoebe's mother, Rhea, was a daemon and had once been able to change how someone felt. Rhea could calm a room instantly before her mental issues started. Phoebe's talent was reading someone's thoughts. If her twin sister had lived through birth, Cassandra would have been a prophetess.

Other tribes or families of daemons had different abilities, traditions, and powers. For their tribe, individuals could only have children with people from the same tribe. Although Phoebe was not part of it yet, her tribe had been gearing up for conflict. With globalization and the movements of different daemons, the old tribal boundaries and agreements had been broken.

Apollo paused for a breath and looked at Phoebe. "Any questions yet?"

Phoebe froze. She had no clue what to think. His entire story would sound completely ludicrous, except she could read minds and her name was a character from mythology. Deciding for the moment to just assume he was truthful, she asked him a question. "So this is the backstory. But when you came to my shop, you said that you needed my help. For what?”

“A Qilin was born.”

“What is a Qilin?” Phoebe frowned. None of this was getting any easier to understand.

“As the myth goes, a Qilin was a creature that resembled a giraffe with dragon-like features. According to legend, a Qilin appeared before the birth of a great leader or wise man. Unfortunately, we are not entirely sure how the Qilin could foretell which person was the new leader.”

“So a giraffe with dragon scales was born?” Phoebe asked.

“That was the myth. In reality, the Qilin is chosen by a random selection of names. For the Chinese daemon, a system of divining blocks is used. They ask the gods if a name is correct and drop the blocks on the ground. The way the divining blocks fall show if the answer is yes or no. About 30 years ago, two parents went through every name they could possibly think of for their unborn daughter. Finally, they threw out Qilin because it was the only name out of thousands that they had yet to say. Although they checked and rechecked the blocks, the answer kept coming up as a yes. Qilin Wang was born about 30 years ago. To find a great leader that will unite our clans or at least end the fighting, we need to find Qilin.”

Phoebe’s mind began racing with many questions but before she could ask a single one, they arrived at the mental institution. Nervous, she let Apollo check in for her and they made their way through the hallways. Sitting in a day room and working at an easel, Phoebe saw a woman with dark auburn hair and dull green eyes. With a start, she realized that this must be her mother. Never had Phoebe felt so certain about anything before. Walking up to the woman, she placed her hand on Rhea's arm.

In a stream, visions and fragments of visions floated across her mind. She saw a man approaching Rhea in a dark alleyway. A silent scream rose from her lips as the man choked Rhea and pulled up her skirt. Trying not to see the vision, Phoebe was locked in place as the man came into Rhea. As Rhea struggled and cried, he lifted his arm to knock her out. The memory ended and a new one filled her mind. In it, Rhea was crying over a cup of tea and staring at a pregnancy test. In quick succession, the birth followed and the stillborn daughter.

Finally, she saw Rhea talking to a little girl who must have been Phoebe. Rhea was trying to hold the baby Phoebe, but the child just kept crying. As soon as the child was put down, the crying would cease. Terrified, Phoebe watched as Rhea realized what was going on. The child was seeing through her memories of the rape and the anguish that followed. Crying, Rhea sat away from the child. The memory broke apart and Phoebe looked up.

In front of her, the real Rhea smiled kindly. "I knew you would come someday, dear. I always hoped to meet you in person."

Phoebe waited a moment to catch her breath. The violence of the rape, the terror of Rhea and the child hanging in the balance were too much for her. She could see why Rhea ended up in a mental institution. Haggardly, she asked, "Is that why you gave me up?"

Rhea nodded. "I didn't want to. Even though you reminded me of him, you were my daughter. But I couldn't keep you from reading my thoughts and you kept seeing the worst event of my life played over and over. There was no way that you could grow up with a normal life after that. I am glad to see the woman that you have become."

Leaning back, Phoebe nodded. "So it is all true then? About the daemons and the Qilin?"

Rhea sighed. "Yes, I am afraid so. That prophecy must be a lot to handle."

"Prophecy?"

Rhea darted her eyes toward Apollo. "You didn't tell her?"

Apollo shook his head. "It wasn't my place. She needed to meet you first and see that what I am saying is real."

Rhea nodded. "Not long after your birth, the ghost of Cassandra visited me. Instead of an infant, she appeared to me as an adult. She told me that the killing of the Qilin would reveal the great leader who would bring peace among the daemons."

Phoebe paused. "So Apollo needs me to find the Qilin so he can kill it? How will that work?"

Turning to Phoebe, Apollo shrugged. "I have narrowed down where the Qilin may be to San Francisco's Chinatown. After her birth, her parents sent her to the United States to hide her. All you need to do is touch the arm of girls that are about 20-30 years old in Chinatown and read their thoughts. From their thoughts, you will be able to find which girl is actually the Qilin."

Phoebe nodded. Everything seemed so strange, but she had lived as an oddity all her life. At least now she had a reason that explained her abilities and why she grew up so alone. "I'm in. Let's go find the Qilin."

Chapter Two

After a day of flying, Phoebe and Apollo finally made it to San Francisco. Alone in the hotel room together, Phoebe eyed Apollo as he walked across the room to her. His tousled blond hair fell across his forehead as he sat down next to her. Touching her arm, he started to say something but stopped when he saw the expression on Phoebe's face. Once physical contact was made, his thoughts entered her mind. Visions of the two of them together and making love flooded through her thoughts. Realizing that she saw his thoughts—and was not trying to pull away—Apollo leaned in to kiss her.

Pressing her into the bed, Apollo started to passionately kiss down her neck. Filled with desire, Phoebe moved to take off his shirt. She threw her dress onto the ground and pulled Apollo toward her. Unable to wait any longer, she pulled him into her. Apollo thrust deep inside her and she moaned for more. Their two bodies rocked in unison on the bed as desire radiated from their bodies. Rolling over, Apollo pulled her body on top of him. Phoebe threw her head back and arched her back so he could go deeper inside of her. Nothing seemed to exist anymore and nothing mattered except continuing. With each thrust, their bodies fell into a rhythm that seemed so natural. It felt like their bodies had once known each other and were now becoming reacquainted.

Without a word from either of them, they simultaneously orgasmed. Phoebe's mind felt like a searing light was passing through it. Pure pleasure caused her body to clench against his uncontrollably in a rhythm. As the orgasm came to an end, Phoebe fell back onto the bed next to him.

Moments passed before either of them could say anything. It seemed so strange to hook up like this, but so right at the same time. Without thinking about it, Apollo began to lazily run his hands along her breasts and stomach. Each touch sent shivers through Phoebe's body.

Rolling over to kiss her belly button, Apollo rested his head on her stomach. "Do you believe in fate, Phoebe?"

Phoebe laughed. "Not really, what makes you ask?"

"It just makes sense. How could a Qilin's death show a leader if there isn't fate? At any rate, I think that you are the person I'm supposed to be with."

This conversation was getting too serious for Phoebe. She had just met him a few days ago. Although they just had sex together, it was not like she expected them to spend the rest of their lives together. Shrugging off his comment, she changed the subject. "When are we going back out to look for the Qilin?"

Getting up, Apollo stood naked before her. Each muscle was taut along his body. For a moment, she wanted to be with him again. Pointing toward the bathroom, he started to speak. "I just need five minutes to shower up and change. I'll be out in just a moment."

Apollo left the room to shower while Phoebe threw on her clothes. She wanted to get some fresh air and a quick cup of coffee before he returned. Exiting the hotel room, she nearly bumped into someone. Glancing up, she saw a man with tan skin and black hair. His eyes flashed good-naturedly at her.

"Oh! I am so sorry, Mr...?"

"Supay. You can call me Supay." He grinned and his teeth flashed a brilliant white across his rugged skin. "Don't worry about it at all. I was just going to get a cup of coffee."

Phoebe smiled. "I was about to do the same thing. Care to walk there with me? My name is Phoebe by the way." She reached out to shake his hand. Supay shook his head.

"I'd love to get a cup of coffee with you, but I don't want to give you my cold, so I will take a rain check on shaking your hand."

Together, they headed toward the cafe. As they walked, Supay became quiet. The small talk they had been carrying on grounded to a halt. Waiting in line for coffee, Phoebe turned to him. "Why are you so quiet all of a sudden? Is there something wrong?"

Motioning toward a table, Supay sat down. "There isn't anything wrong exactly. I just..." He gazed off. For a moment, Phoebe thought he forgot that he was talking to her. "I am here for the same thing that you are. I know about the Qilin."

Phoebe's jaw dropped. "Are you a daemon? How do you know about me? Do you plan on killing the Qilin first?"

Supay shook his head. "Hopefully, I will stop the Qilin from dying at all. She's just a girl and doesn't deserve to die. Leaders will come and go without her death. Everyone seems so sure that fate has demanded this girl die for the greater good. Human sacrifice for a cause—in this case, murder—seems so archaic. I know about you because all the other hunters for the Qilin talk about you. Your special skills make it possible to uncover where the Qilin has been hiding."

"But, Supay... you make it sound so terrible. If it is something that has to happen and it stops all of the daemons from fighting, isn't her death a good thing? Apollo doesn't seem like some master villain. He really wants to help."

Supay chuckled darkly. "No, Apollo is convinced that he is doing this for the best reasons. The other hunters are doing it for power, recognition, or out of the same misguided goal of helping the greater good." He stood up to leave. "I just hope you don't get hurt in the search. There are other ways for someone to become a leader. You don't have to be involved in such a distasteful enterprise. I'll give you my card. Call this number if you need help." Without thinking about it, he reached out his hand with his card. Their fingers touched for a moment. Phoebe saw the image of a dog's teeth closing around a frisbee. Confused by this brief vision, she started to say something. When she looked up again, Supay was gone.

Back in the room, Apollo was just getting out of the shower. As he put on his clothes, Phoebe broached him with a question. "So what you were saying about fate earlier... do you really believe in it?"

Apollo smiled. "Of course. Just think of the myriad of possibilities that brought us together. To find the Qilin, I needed exactly you. You happened to be from the same daemon family, which is unlikely at best. Our daemon family happens to be one of the few that can only have children with other members of the same tribe. To top it off, I like you. What are the chances?"

Phoebe frowned. She forgot that he was talking about her fate earlier and not just fate. "But the Qilin? Does this girl really have to die? I understand that there is a prophecy, but can't we change it?"

Shaking his head, Apollo threw on his jacket. "The Qilin has known since birth that this would happen. Fate demands that she die and a leader be revealed that will bring about the peace of the daemons. Her death will prevent other deaths from happening. It may be distasteful, but everyone knows that this will have to happen at some point." Motioning toward the door, Apollo grabbed his keys. "Come on, we need to start looking."

Chapter Three

Weeks passed and Phoebe could not manage to find the Qilin. She spent each day wandering around Chinatown touching girls on their back or shaking hands. Apollo spent the time waiting in a cafe while she wandered the streets. In all honesty, part of her did not want to actually find the Qilin. Phoebe could not reconcile the views of Apollo and Supay. She understood that the death of the Qilin could bring about a better world, but sacrificing one girl for that goal was inhumane. She found her own feelings conflicted and perplexing.

Rounding a corner, Phoebe came across a jade and precious stone shop. In the window, jade necklaces hung in rows. Tired of searching for the Qilin, Phoebe went in. She had been eyeing a green jade necklace that was shaped like a dragon for a while. Each day, she passed the shop and never had time to go in.

Entering the dimly lit store, Phoebe glanced around. All the walls were filled with a range of talismans and jade. A giant jade Buddha sat on an altar along the back of the room. An old curtain hid the door to the back of the shop. Behind a counter, a beautiful young girl smiled at Phoebe.

"May I help you find what are you looking for today?" she asked. Her voice had a slight accent like so many people in Chinatown.

"I was looking at that jade dragon necklace in the window. Can I try it on?"

The girl gazed back at Phoebe with wide, almond-shaped eyes. "I think it may be too large for your neckline. Here, let me read your tarot cards. I can help you figure out which type of necklace suits you."

Phoebe shrugged. Why not, she thought. The girl shuffled the cards on the counter and set them down for Phoebe to cut. Laying out the cards one-by-one, the girl fell silent. She pressed her mouth into a thin line and closed her eyes for a moment.

Worried, Phoebe stretched her arm toward the girl to see if she was all right. As she touched her arm, visions flashed through her mind. Phoebe saw what the girl saw in the cards. Images floated through Phoebe's mind of a sword stabbing the girl. To the side, a vision of Phoebe looked on during the death. Trouble in love, confusion, and an ultimate decision floated through her mind.

Startled, Phoebe pulled her arm back. The girl must be the Qilin. Coughing, the girl looked up. "It's okay, I'm not afraid. I know who you are now. Your role is important, but you are not to blame for my eventual death. I forgive you for what you are required to do."

Aghast, Phoebe took a step back. "How can you accept it so easily? I still don't know what to do."

Qilin shook her head. "I have been waiting for this all my life. My parents tried to hide me from death, but I have always known. I have lived decades longer than I should have. If someone must be involved in my death, I am glad it is you. I was afraid of what would happen if a cruel or sadistic person was the ultimate cause. Despite accepting my fate, I will still fight back." She reached for Phoebe's hand and closed her eyes. "I can see... Apollo? He is the one with you? Excellent choice. Few others could take me on."

Letting go of Phoebe's hand, Qilin walked to the wall of the shop and selected a green jade necklace. On it was an obscure Chinese character. The jade looked old and worn. Dusting it off, Qilin placed it around Phoebe's neck. "This will help you in the coming years. Although you want the dragon, it does not suit your future or your temperament."

Phoebe fingered the jade necklace. "It is beautiful. How much is it?"

Qilin shook her head. "No charge. It is the right fit for you and you need it." Leaning forward, she kissed Phoebe on the cheek sadly. "Good luck. I know my death is near and that it has been decreed by fate. After I am gone, do not lose hope. Although fate exists, few people can ever know how it truly works out. Things that seem fated often are not. Even prophesies tend to work out in strange ways. You are going to have a lot of confusion in your life and with romance. Continue to choose what you feel is right because that will lead to your ultimate fate."

Phoebe stepped back and put her hand on the door of the shop. "I am sorry Qilin. Good luck. I hope it ends up working out in a better way."

Qilin nodded and smiled wanly. "I understand. Good luck to you as well."

Leaving the shop, Phoebe walked slowly back to where Apollo was waiting for her. She was no longer sure about what to do. Qilin had told her that it was all right, but she also told Phoebe to listen to her conscience. Sighing, Phoebe entered the café. She would tell Apollo and ask him to protect Qilin instead of killing her.

Apollo looked up as Phoebe entered. "Hey beautiful, how was today's search?" He stood up to give her a kiss before sitting down.

Phoebe took a shaky breath before speaking. "I found her. She works at a jade shop."

Apollo stared at her without saying anything for a moment. After he managed to overcome his shock, he jumped up and gave her another kiss.

"That's amazing! We have to go back to the hotel and prepare. Does she suspect that you know?" Grabbing her by the arm, he started to lead her out of the shop.

"She knows. We talked. She isn't going to go anywhere though. Qilin thinks that this is her fate. She will fight back, but she won't leave." Phoebe bit her lip. She didn't want to tell him what Qilin had said about

Phoebe's future. "Apollo, are you sure we have to kill her? Can't we protect her instead or just leave her alone? You could still be a leader and help bring daemons to peace without her death."

Apollo shook his head. "That would be impossible. This is how it has to happen. The Qilin must die for the leader to be revealed. I don't make the rules; I only play by them."

Entering the hotel room, Apollo's mood suddenly changed. More than anything, he suddenly wanted to be inside Phoebe. He threw her against the wall and pinned her hands above her head. Surprised, Phoebe tried to writhe away. Apollo's grip grew tighter around her wrists and pressed against her. All of her movement and struggle to get away only turned him on more.

Pushing him away forcefully, Phoebe watched as Apollo fell onto the bed. She was not going to let him control her like that. Grabbing a knife that sat on the table, she motioned toward some rope. "Tie your feet to the bed."

As Apollo willingly consented, Phoebe ruffled through the bag of supplies that Apollo packed for the Qilin hunt. Grabbing a pair of handcuffs, she threw them toward Apollo. "Put these on."

After Apollo put the handcuffs on, Phoebe strode across the room. Apollo lay back on the bed willingly as she ran her knife against his flesh. His skin quivered as he simultaneously wanted her touch, but feared the knife. Phoebe ran it down the chiseled center of his abs. Unzipping his pants, she took just his head into her mouth and teased it. Stopping abruptly, she leaned back.

"You want me. What if I make you wait? What if I just sit here and make you suffer?" She felt aroused as she watched him quiver in front of her. His cock was jumping with every movement of his body.

Minutes passed in silence as she waited. Walking across the room, she stood in plain view of him. Slowly, painstakingly, she unbuttoned her shirt and pulled it off. Her breasts popped out of her bra and bounced against her chest in an inviting motion. On the bed, Apollo could barely contain himself. Phoebe slipped out of her pants and stood before him. All that remained on her body was the jade necklace. Slowly, she slipped it off.

Moving over to the bed, she straddled his body and gently lowered herself on to him. At first, she just teased his head. Driven mad by her teasing, Apollo thrust his hips upwards so that he entered her fully. Phoebe gasped. The pleasure of having him inside her made her unable to continue teasing him any longer. She unlocked his handcuffs hurriedly and untied his legs. Throwing off his restraints, Apollo threw her onto her stomach on the table. Thrusting back inside her, his motions became quick and lacked rhythm. There was no time to slow down or make love. This was just violent, unbridled passion.

Phoebe pulled against the edge of the table to keep balance and to push her body harder against his. The curtains in front of her face were open, but she didn't care. All she wanted was to orgasm. She could feel an orgasm approaching, but couldn't quite reach it. Phoebe screamed in frustration.

Pulling away from Apollo, she shoved the table out of the way. Apollo lifted her body against the window and wrapped her legs around him. Pushing into her again, his cock quivered. He could feel himself growing close to orgasm, but he wanted to wait for Phoebe. Their naked bodies caused steam to develop on the window.

If someone were to pass outside, they would just see Phoebe's back moving against the wall. The danger excited Phoebe and pushed her desire further. Pulling him against her, she clutched his body against her and stopped him from moving as her orgasm started. Apollo's hand on her head clutched as he started to orgasm with her and yanked her head back. Gasping in ecstasy, Phoebe collapsed as her body shook from the violence of the orgasm. Unable to even draw the energy to move to the bed, the pair fell onto the floor together.

"So tomorrow..." Phoebe paused and caught her breath. "You kill Qilin?"

Apollo held her hand and kissed each finger. His blue eyes looked into hers. Although she tried not to read his thoughts, she could feel the excitement welling up inside him and it worried her.

"Tomorrow, I kill the Qilin."

-To be continued in Book 2-

If you enjoyed this title, I would appreciate your leaving a review of the book. Good reviews encourage an author to write as well as help books to sell. Good reviews can be just a few short sentences describing what you liked about the book without having a spoiler. If you could spend 30 seconds writing a review, I would appreciate it: you can review this title right now at your favorite retailer.

Here is a preview of the **next story** you may enjoy:

WALKING OUT of the hotel room, Phoebe jumped back in surprise. Her dog, Ace, ran up to her. "Ace! What are you doing here?" She leaned down to pet him. "Come inside with me and we will get you something to eat."

Bringing him inside with her, she glanced over at Apollo. She met his questioning eyes with a shrug. "I have no clue how he got here. It seems impossible, but here he is."

Apollo shrugged. "Weirder things have happened. I guess we can just bring him along with us. Having him could help." Standing up, he grabbed the bag of weapons and restraints. Together, they left the room and got in the car.

Parking near the jade shop, the pair sipped coffee as they waited for Qilin to close the shop. They inched the car along behind her as she went to a park. The sunlight was quickly fading away and few people were in the park. Quickly, they got out of the car and followed Qilin into a clearing. Although they walked in absolute silence, Qilin turned around.

"I knew you were there. This is your last chance to turn back. Are you ready?" She widened her stance and stood confidently in front of them. Phoebe stepped back so that Apollo could do what he came for.

Grabbing a dagger out of the bag, Apollo nodded. "I am ready if you are." As soon as he finished the sentence, Qilin became a blazing ball of fire. Flames radiated from her arms and curled into balls within her hands. Throwing the fire at Apollo, she moved forward. Apollo ducked the flames and tried to get into an offensive position.

Ace whined next to Phoebe. Leaning down, she patted his head reassuringly. In reality, she was shaking in fear. Still unused to the world of daemons, the fiery daemon before her was a frightening surprise. She felt less terrible about the possibility of Qilin's death. The daemon before her was far from defenseless. Before this moment, how many other potential leaders had tried to kill Qilin and failed?

Qilin threw another ball of fire and it singed Apollo's heels. The grass in the clearing was quickly becoming torched by their fight. Ball after ball of fire was thrown and Apollo managed to shrug it off without any difficulties. Unfortunately, he was unable to stand long enough to get close to her. It was too late when he realized that he should have just used a gun. Rolling away from another ball of fire, he quickly darted in the opposite direction. The sudden change of direction surprised Qilin, and she let the ball of fire go too soon. It released from her hand and flew directly toward Phoebe. Apollo either did not notice where the fire was headed or did not care. He adjusted his stance and lifted the dagger behind his head to throw it.

If you enjoyed this sample then look for **The Shifter - The Daemon Paranormal Romance Chronicles, Book 2.**

Here is a preview of **another story** you may enjoy:

Awareness - The Mind Talker Paranormal Romance Series, Book 1

"SO SEXY…"

"God I'd love to do her…"

"I wonder if I could find that outfit in my size…"

Ananda had to fight laughter, curling an errant lock of dark auburn hair around her finger as she fought through the crowd of people around her. Laughing for no reason, at least none that could be seen by the general population, is typically frowned upon and usually makes finding friends much more difficult. This she had learned the hard way thanks to the cruelty of middle school students and their need to be popular. Still, it never ceased to surprise her how many inane thoughts humans regularly had running through their minds. Sometimes, Ananda had to totally isolate herself in order to get a moment's rest, particularly when surrounded by the chatter from all directions. Her honey-colored eyes flitted back and forth as she scanned the mass of people around her, thoughts flying into her mind in rapid succession.

It wasn't like Ananda couldn't turn it off, her ability to hear other people's thoughts. When she was younger, it was definitely more difficult to sift through the roiling voices and images that seemed to seep into her head with little direction or effort. At first when her ability manifested at the tender age of eleven, Ananda was terrified as were her parents, who were ignorant of such abilities. Her older brother Ryan had been a source of strength and stability for her as the family went from one psychologist to another attempting to find a reason or cure for the 'voices' Ananda claimed to hear. It was he, who helped her find a center in order to control the flow of voices until they were barely more than a brush against her mind. Ryan's move across the country for school was rough though manageable for Ananda as she began to explore the range of her ability and discover the fun she could have with it. Her moral compass wasn't as low as some, so she didn't use it for anything that would get her ahead academically, but she did use it to benefit herself and those she loved.

"Ananda, over here!"

Refocusing on the crowd around her, Ananda spotted one of the few people she could actually call a friend. Kerri wasn't what anyone would call quiet. Her small stature and pixie-like features made it seem as if she could be blown away by a single puff of air, but her exuberant personality and sharp, sometimes biting, use of sarcasm made her seem larger than her thin frame. Bright red hair the color of the sunset and eyes that seemed to change color depending on her mood completed the full package that was Kerri Donahue. However, it wasn't just Kerri's larger-than-life personality that drew Ananda in, it was more of what Kerri didn't exude. Her mind was quiet.

No matter how intently Ananda poked and prodded, she could only get a faint hum and vague feelings from her friend's mind. Rather than being unnerved by that, Ananda felt a sense of relief at finally finding one person who didn't give her a headache just by being around so often. Even with her brother Ryan, Ananda had to occasionally leave in order to calm her own mind and get some relief from his mind's 'voice.' The fact that Kerri seemed oblivious to how special she was sometimes made Ananda pause and wonder if she was the only one out there with a strange ability. Was there someone out there like Professor X who was searching for people like her? Was there a way to find others? Or did she spend way too much time reading comic books and hoping that some parts of those stories were influenced by actual facts?

If you enjoyed this sample then look for **Awareness - The Mind Talker Paranormal Romance Series, Book 1**.

Other Books by Darla Dunbar

- The Romeo Alpha BBW Paranormal Shifter Romance Series

- Romeo Alpha Blood Lines Romance

- The Alpha Feud BBW Paranormal Shifter Romance Series

- The Alpha Packed BBW Paranormal Shifter Romance Series

- The Mind Talker Paranormal Romance Series

- The Leather Satchel Paranormal Romance Series

Get the latest update on new releases from the author at:

https://darladunbar.com/newsletter/

About the Author - Darla Dunbar

Darla has been interested in paranormal romance since she was a teenager in high school. It was then that she discovered she could fulfill her fantasies through her writing.

Observing people and human behavior in the area of romance has always been one of her favorite pastimes. Combining that with an overactive imagination is a sure fire way of coming up with interesting themes.

Connect with Darla Dunbar

I really appreciate you reading my book! Here are my social media coordinates:

Friend me on Facebook: https://www.facebook.com/darladunbar/

Follow me on Twitter: https://twitter.com/DarlDunbar

Check me out on Goodreads: https://www.goodreads.com/author/show/8425857.Darla_Dunbar

Subscribe to my newsletter: https://darladunbar.com/newsletter/

Visit my website: https://darladunbar.com/